Tidy Up, Winnie!

LAURA OWEN & KORKY PAUL

OXFORD

Helping your child to read

Before they start

* Talk about the back cover blurb. How does your child think Winnie might get down again when she's trapped in a bubble?
* Look at the cover pictures. Do they give any clues about what might happen in the stories?

During reading

* Let your child read at their own pace – don't worry if it's slow. They could read silently, or read to you out loud.
* Help them to work out words they don't know by saying each sound out loud and then blending them to say the word, e.g. *t-oa-d-s-t-oo-l, toadstool.*
* If your child still struggles with a word, just tell them the word and move on.
* Give them lots of praise for good reading!

After reading

* Look at page 48 for some fun activities.

Contents

OXFORD
UNIVERSITY PRESS

Great Clarendon Street, Oxford OX2 6DP
Oxford University Press is a department of the University of Oxford.
It furthers the University's objective of excellence in research, scholarship,
and education by publishing worldwide. Oxford is a registered trade mark
of Oxford University Press in the UK and in certain other countries

"Winnie's Bubble Trouble" was first published in *Winnie Goes Batty* 2010
"Winnie Gets Bossy" was first published in *Winnie on Patrol* 2010
This edition published 2018

British Library Cataloguing in Publication Data

Data available

ISBN: 978-0-19-276523-9

1 3 5 7 9 10 8 6 4 2

Printed in China

Paper used in the production of this book is a natural,
recyclable product made from wood grown in sustainable forests.
The manufacturing process conforms to the environmental
regulations of the country of origin.

Acknowledgements
With thanks to Catherine Baker for editorial support

Winnie's Bubble Trouble

⭐ Chapter ⭐ One

Glug-glug-slurp. Winnie was drinking fizzy froggle-pop.

Scrunch-munch-gulp. Wilbur was eating crispy mouse tails.

Bip-wiggle-bop. Winnie and Wilbur were both in the kitchen, singing and dancing along to the very loud music.

Winnie and Wilbur were having a party, just for the two of them. They had pumpkin pizza, toad on toast and crunchy cabbage crisps to munch. They had balloons and streamers. It was a lot of fun!

Winnie and Wilbur went to bed very late that night. Wilbur went straight to sleep. But Winnie didn't.

Snore went Wilbur. **Snore-snore-SNORE!**

"Oh, please shush, Wilbur!" said Winnie,
putting her hands over her ears.

Snore-snore-snore. SNORE-splutter!

"No!" moaned Winnie. "I can't sleep with
that noise!"

Snore-SNORE-snore.

Winnie put her pillow over her head, but she couldn't get to sleep. She was still wide awake. And she stayed wide awake for the rest of the night.

⭐ Chapter ⭐
Two

When the sun came up, Winnie got up too.
She felt very tired. She tried to make Wilbur
a toadstool toasty for breakfast. But she
didn't watch what she was doing.

Soon, flames were coming from the cooker.

"Meeow!" went Wilbur. He spat the burnt
toadstool toasty out. Winnie didn't want to
eat it either.

So they opened a can of beans and had them for breakfast instead.

Then Winnie tried to tidy up all the mess left over from the party.

Boom! The vacuum cleaner exploded.

Bang-sploosh! The washing machine broke down.

"Mee-hee-hee-ow!" laughed Wilbur.

There was mess everywhere! Then Winnie slipped in a puddle of water.

Slip-crash! She knocked over a pile of plates and pans.

Bang!

Clang!

Smash!

"Oh, soggy slug bottoms!" cried Winnie, covering her ears. "I wish I could float away from all this noise, and go somewhere calm and quiet." She waved her wand.

"Abracadabra!"

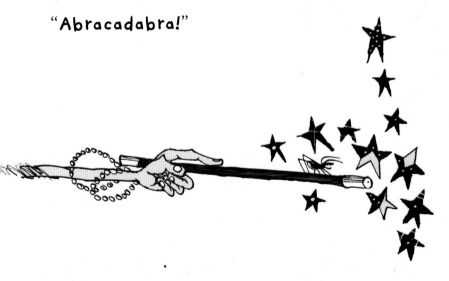

At once, Winnie was inside a giant
bubble. It floated silently out through the
window, and up into the sky.

"Ah," said Winnie. She closed her eyes and
snoozed for a while as she floated up and up.

16

When she opened her eyes, she saw birds and planes passing, but she couldn't hear them. "Perfect!" said Winnie.

Then she looked down. Her house looked tiny, far down below. Wilbur was only the size of a flea.

"Oooh!" said Winnie. "I'm too high up in the sky! Get me down!" But Winnie couldn't wave her wand, in case she popped the bubble. "Help!" she said, feeling a bit panicky. "HELP!"

No sound came out of the bubble. But a small sound came from Winnie, inside the bubble. **Parp!**

"Whoops!" said Winnie.

The bubble got a little bit bigger.

"Pongy-wongy!" said Winnie. "Why did I eat those beans for breakfast? Wilbur, save me!"

Wilbur was down on the ground. He saw Winnie's bubble floating high up in the sky. He was worried.

"Meeow!" he called. He knew he had to get up there to help Winnie – but how? He didn't have wings! And he couldn't fly Winnie's broom. But Wilbur did have balloons left over from the party.

Wilbur grabbed lots of balloon strings. He tied some to his tail and held tight to the others. Then he began to slowly float up into the sky.

⭐ Chapter ⭐ Three

Up, up, up went Wilbur until he was next to Winnie's bubble. Winnie was waving and moving her mouth.

"Get me out of this pongy bubble!" she shouted.

But how could Wilbur burst the bubble without letting Winnie fall from the sky?

"Meeow!" Wilbur had an idea. He let go of one balloon.

"Wilbur!" called Winnie, as Wilbur and his balloons sank lower. But now Wilbur's balloons were like a cushion under Winnie's bubble. That way, Winnie could pop her bubble and be safe. She poked and poked with her wand and **pop!** the pongy-wongy bubble burst. Winnie landed on the balloons.

"Ah, fresh air!" she said. But Winnie was heavy and the balloons quickly began to sink. "Whoops!"

"**Tweet tweet!**"

"What's happening . . ." began Winnie as a flock of big-beaky birdies flew alongside her.

"A tweety-tweet treat!" went the birds.
They thought Wilbur's brightly coloured
balloons looked like juicy fruit. So the birds
started to peck the balloons.

Peck-peck-pop-pop-pop!

One by one, the balloons all went **pop!**
Winnie and Wilbur started to fall. Winnie
flapped her arms, trying to fly. It didn't
work! Just then, Winnie remembered
that she had her wand.

"**Abracadabra!**" she shouted.

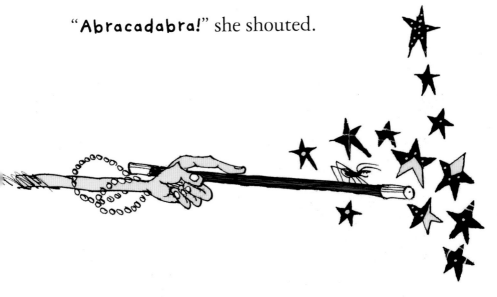

At once, a big umbrella appeared.
Winnie and Wilbur floated down slowly
and landed gently in a lovely, soft, flowery
meadow.

"**Tweet-tweet!**" sang some birdies.

"I've had enough of birdies for one day," said Winnie. "But at least I'm safe on the ground!"

"Meeow," said Wilbur. **Yawn!**

Yawn! "I'm tired, too!" said Winnie.

So they settled down to sleep in the long grass. But after a moment, Wilbur began to snore again.

Snore-snore SNORE!

"Not again!" cried Winnie. But she was so tired, that soon she was snoring too.

SNORE! SNORE-SNORE! Grunt-grunt-grunt. SNOOOOORE!

So it was only the birdies who had to cover their ears.

Winnie
Gets Bossy

★ Chapter ★ One

Winnie was watching the telly. Her dirty boots were up on the armchair. She was eating chocolate cockroaches, and spilling them everywhere.

Scratch-tug! Wilbur was happily scratching Winnie's chair. His claws were ripping the cloth and tugging out all of the stuffing.

"Look at this, Wilbur," said Winnie. "That man is showing how you can make your room look fresh and new just by moving your furniture around!"

Winnie had an idea. She jumped up, spilling her fizzy froggle-pop. "Let's try it, Wilbur!" she said. "Let's move the big table over there."

Winnie and Wilbur pushed and pushed, but the table didn't want to move.

Scrape-screech! went Winnie.

Puff-pant! went Wilbur.

The table was leaving scrape marks on the floor.

"Oh, fish flippers, look at that!" said Winnie. "Pass me that rug, Wilbur."

Wilbur and Winnie put the rug over the marks, but …

Trip-smash!

Winnie tripped over the rug.

"Humph!" Winnie pulled out her wand. "Listen to me, furniture! If you're going to behave as if you're alive, then I'll make you really come alive! Then you can move yourselves to where I want!"

Winnie waved her wand.

"Abracadabra!"

Instantly the furniture sat up straight.

"Oooh, that's better!" said Winnie. "Right then, chairs, tidy yourselves up. Off you go!"

At once, the dining chairs marched neatly into place around the table.

"Brilliant!" said Winnie. She put a tin of polish and an old vest on the table. "Polish yourself, please, table!"

One of the table's legs grabbed the polish tin. Another leg grabbed the vest. Then the table polished itself, just like a person brushing their hair.

Winnie went up to her bedroom.

"Bed, make yourself!" she said.

Winnie's bed did a little jiggle, and all the covers went neat and tidy.

"Curtains, draw yourselves!" said Winnie.

Swish-swoosh!

"Ha ha! Do it again!" said Winnie.

Swish-swoosh!

"This is fun!" laughed Winnie.

Chapter Two

Winnie went back downstairs. "Hatstand, do a disco dance!" she said. And it did.

Wilbur pointed at the armchair. So Winnie told it, "Chair, dance the hokey cokey for us!"

The fat-bellied armchair tried to dance, but its legs were too stumpy.

"Mee-hee-hee-ow!" laughed Wilbur.

Suddenly all the furniture started to rumble-grumble.

"Oooh, look!" said Winnie. The armchair was getting crosser and crosser. It puffed up, and stamped its little legs, and waved its fat little arms. Then it ran towards Wilbur.

"Hiss!" went Wilbur, and then he ran off too. Wilbur leaped onto the table, but – uh-oh! – the table flipped onto its back. It grabbed Wilbur with all its legs, as if it was a spider and Wilbur was a fly.

"Meeow!" yelled Wilbur.

"Oooh, Wilbur, the furniture is cross with you for scratching it!" said Winnie.

But the furniture was cross with Winnie, too. The fat-bellied armchair ran up fast behind her, making her sit down in it very suddenly. Then it wrapped its arms around Winnie's waist.

"Oooh, help! Dining chairs, help me!" shouted Winnie. But those chairs just crossed their arms.

"Cupboard?" said Winnie. The cupboard turned its back.

"Oh, please!" wailed Winnie. "I promise I won't make you do anything you don't want to ever again!"

The armchair let her go. "Phew!" said Winnie.

The table set Wilbur free. "Meeow!" he said, happily.

But the stool marched over to the front door and opened it.

Creeeeeak!

Then the television, the bed, the chairs, and all the other furniture marched out of the door and away.

"They've left home!" cried Winnie.

Winnie and Wilbur sat on the floor to eat their supper.

"We'll have to sleep on the floor, too," said Winnie. "There are lots of ants and spiders, so it could be a tickly night!"

Chapter Three

Winnie was right. The floor was hard and very cold.

"Oh, Wilbur," said Winnie. "I liked our old furniture the way it was. Oh, silly me!"

Then, suddenly, there was a **bang-bang-bang!** from the front door. "**Winnieeee!**" yelled the doorbell.

"Ouch!" Winnie got up and walked stiffly to the door.

Creeeeeak! She pulled the door open. And in marched Winnie's bed, her television, her table, her chairs, her bath …

"Hooray! Welcome home!" said Winnie, clapping her hands.

"Hiss!" Wilbur leaped onto the windowsill.

"Why did you come home, my furniture friends?" asked Winnie.

The hatstand pointed outside. It was stormy and wet and cold and dark out there.

"I see," said Winnie. "Well, just sit wherever you want to be. I'll magic you back to your proper selves. **Abracadabra!**"

Some things ended up in rather odd places.

"You can come down now, Wilbur," said Winnie. "And we can go to sleep in a proper bed, even though it's in the kitchen."

Winnie sat on the bed, but she got a shock. It was wet and full of leaves – and it had a baby hedgehog sleeping in it!

But Wilbur found something soft and
dry and warm to sleep on. It was Winnie's
tummy. He purred, and his claws went in
and out.

"Ouch! Now I know how the furniture
feels!" said Winnie. "Wilbur, put those
claws away!"

After reading activities

Quick quiz

See how fast you can answer these questions! Look back at the stories if you can't remember.

1) In "Winnie's Bubble Trouble", how does Wilbur get up into the sky?
2) In "Winnie's Bubble Trouble", what does Winnie use to pop the bubble?
3) In "Winnie Gets Bossy", what did Winnie tell the hatstand and the chair to do?

1) he uses balloons left over from the party. 2) her wand.
3) she told them to dance.

Talk about it!

★ Would it be fun to float up in a bubble like Winnie, or would you be scared? What might you see if you were way up in the sky?

48